The Short Story

of

Miss Lacy

Jimmy Swagger

Copyright © 2024 by Jimmy Swagger

All rights reserved. No part of this book can be reproduced in any form without permission from the author.

To request permission, contact Travis T. Pack at jimmyswagger75author@gmail.com

Cover design and Interior formatting: Ailadesigns.com

ISBN 979-8-218-40857-2

Published by: Selfpublishinghelp.net

Table of Contents

Who Is the True Idiot?

Missy Lacy: she was your typical street hustler. She loved everything about the streets. She controlled her work schedule, chose her daily attire, decided where and when to conduct her business, and determined her hourly pay. Good stuff, right? Well, some folks look down on hookers as if they were just crackheads rolling from one bed to another without a plan.

Well, they are actually crackheads. Yeah, so there is half a truth there. But, think for a second. Who's the real idiot here? Is it the mindless sheep who go to a dead-end job they hate, that mindless fuck who is then required to wear some cheese-dick uniform they hate, only to go home and fuck only himself through Pornhub. His wife cannot stand him, which is why she fucks her psychiatrist, who supplies her with unlimited pills so she can numb her worthless waste of a life away. Then only to do it again and again and again till life shows them the exit.

Now, let's think. Who is the true entrepreneur, and who is the worthless stupid fuck? The whore or the cheese DICK? Well, she enjoyed cock way before the start of the soon-to-be pumping business. So this was just a perk. She handled all of the above addictions like a champ - alcoholism, drug addiction, and sexual addiction. She just enjoyed them all! They say one should pursue what they love and be the best at it! Well, Miss Lacy really dick-sucks a mean cock. Most men didn't last more than a moment. So I would say that makes her qualify to get some CHW awards, right? Ok, she used to have a pimp, but she put in the hours to advance her position! So who's the idiot here?

Fred

Fred is a class act; a six foot seven inch monster. This piece of shit molested his first little girl when he was just 15 years old. He was all the cheesedick a person could stand - tall, ugly,sweaty, piece of shit. I mean, think about the worst locker rooms you've ever smelled, or those sweaty balls that radiate a specially ripe mix of balls mixed with asshole juices. Well, this winner happened upon Miss Lacy one fateful night in Chicago, in the trashiest of motels, a really nice establishment owned by some middle eastern sheik wannabe who was just living that American dream— one hourly rental at a time. So, Fred knew how to find his fix populated corner on a dark Chicago night. It was special night And Fred really felt it. They say that when you are this close to evil, only evil itself can feel glee. Oh, he felt it like a child feels on Christmas morning. Only that this 2 a.m. morning in that lovely Chicago morning was not for Santa Claus show up But it was the star of the night. Miss Lacy and all of her elves. HO HO HO…. Well, Fred felt his ass had a bounce in his step. Then he saw her.

The Encounter

Ok, I don't think staring at a large shit in the toilet for hours could beat this stare that happened. Their eyes met… love at first sight! She knew how to rule a man and wield him like a 9mm. Through that little, tiny princess pole he possessed in his pants.

She took him to Akbar's beautiful establishment. This is the kind of place where Yelp and Expedia don't even have a comment section. They got room 13 to celebrate their union. She put a fucking on that tiny cock that melted him like butter. He was hooked.

Now, we didn't discuss Miss Lacy; this bitch has the darkest soul in existence. She was on the rewards program of "RAPE AND ABUSE R US" she made black holes blush. A real jewel. On her Facebook page under hobbies TORTURE-MURDER-CUTLERY COLLECTIONS-COOKING CORPSES-…. My personal favorite... ANAL RAPING! Good stuff.

This bitch had a taste for blood, and her hobbies followed her skill set. Well, these two were about to clean the street better than Sheriff Arpaio. Let's see murder, mayhem, love, money, and sex. We are about to start this shitshow.

Jonathan

Ok, Jonathan is your typical teenager. Always studying tits and asses from behind the screen. He thinks 22 inches of cock is what women crave. I mean, this kid has ordered everything. Cock rings, penis pumps—anything that can get him closer to being

John Holmes. Well, I cannot blame him. His father left when he was 5. There was never a real male influence other than that computer screen. Think about that. Internet raising the children! Wow, that's scary.

Anyway, no dad. The mother? She's not much better. She went to internet-based sites to find a man. That's funny. The only thing there was the trolls who only thought what Jonathan thought: giant cock gets the prize. So, mommy took a pussy pounding daily. As a child, that's all he heard all the time! Ohh, ohh, ohhh, you're cocks, so big, baby. Imagine that!

Well, this kid's friends were obviously into the same shit. So, they devised a plan and headed down to that same corner, that fucking piece of shit Fred hobbled down too. What a fuck he was! They decided to go be pornstars with a hooker. Oh, this would be the worst decision of their soon-to-be short lives. One last porn hub viewing for these kids, then follow the yellow brick road to Hell!

The Encounter Part 2

So here we go!

How exciting that we finally get to see Miss Lacy in action! She is one hell of an evil cunt. Her soul left her body a long time ago. The only thing that remained was a shell and the darkness.

Ok, back to Miss Lacy. Well, she was on a mission of blood and gore. It was the only thing she had left to smile about. As she and Fred occupied that dark corner, she saw the rich kids SUV pull up ... *Bingo!!!*.... not only a good time, but exactly what she needed in her life. Young cock. The good stuff, and four of them! Man, she couldn't have prayed any harder for this.

Now, mind you, she and Fred knew exactly what they were doing. As Fred approached the teenagers, he advised them of Miss Lacy. That's the one they wanted. As if he were a devil on their shoulder! So hook, line, sinker, they approached her.

They said to her, "We would like to fuck you."

Miss Lacy said, "Oh boys, are all of you just for me?"

They all turned to one another, smiling and giggling, unaware that all they were doing was bringing joy to her. Destroying innocence was like a crack to her. Ultimate pleasure.

"So, you boys want to go upstairs," she said. They all started fumbling for cash. 20s flying on the ground.

Fuck Fest

Ok, are you ready? Here we go!!!

Miss Lacy had Fred go up first. As she walked up to Akbar, Fred said, "Oh Miss Lacy, these boys are too young. I don't need the heat." Lacy snapped back at him, "Shut the fuck up. We need a regular room."

They started passing cash….As they walked down Akbar's fine housing hallways, the guys began to chuckle and snicker at everything a teenager would do at a prom. This was no prom though.. this was a death march that was conducted by our special girl, Miss Lacy! She was waving a conductor's wand as high and rhythmic as the tune that sang aloud in her mind. Yes, that muscle between her ears - Miss Lacy's mind. This mind was not a take-her-home kind of girl's mind. This mind was one that made the Joker from Batman seem to be as normal as a Jehovah witness at your door on an early Saturday morning, bringing his anvil of beliefs.

As she pranced, almost skipping forward and spinning in joy, hands raised and a tune they misunderstood for seductive dancing. Oh, she was dancing—not for what these boys could ever imagine. They saw her body as a porn exhibit. Oh, how far from the truth! It was like a Venus flytrap.

She knew the level of her 100 pounds, not of strength in muscle, oh no. Her 100 pounds were stronger than the largest black diamond, indestructible, and as dark and beautiful as an individual could only lust for. She spun to grab the handle of room 13. Let the fuckfest begin!

The Fucking Symphony

As Miss Lacy spun this final time to the door handle, it would be the last time these boys would be given the chance to walk through the opening we know as a door. Doors are so mysterious….?…are they rectangles?

What is a rectangle? A deformed square, right? It's a stretched-out, imperfect square? Whoever picked that shape for a door? Was there someone who sat there and said, Let's trim the sides of a square down to enter a building? I mean, really. There are many different types of doors, from both physical and mental point of view. Not a portal, but a door. And who decided it needed a circular device—a knob to turn—to enter this imperfect shape? Well, tonight we will unlock a room and unlock your mind for a true Fuck Fest. Yes, this is going to be the **Devil's Symphony**!

Everything a man could only foresee as a true Fuck Fest. As that knob jiggled, Fred dove in the one place, no one but Miss Lacy would visit the restroom! There is no place for anyone there tonight. The only washing for these boys would be the washing of their fears, blood, and terror for the one and only Miss Lacy.

She could only throw the first boy on the bed. As the other boys watched, their little power poles rose to attention! As she stood there, she began to hum; the symphony had begun!

First act. She took her halter top slowly over the first shoulder. As it rose, the boys blood to their members flowed as fast as Shawn White on a downslope. She twisted, humming, and then the first of her unbelievable sexy tits showed up to the party. The nipple glistened as the North Star led the wise men to baby Jesus. She wasn't bringing the games Jesus brought; she was bringing hers. Not a game like morality or repentance but a more simplistic one, one as simple as raw pure fucking. Her rules, her game! Do not pass go head straight to the fuck zone collect 200 dollars !

She let that breast hang out and was it ever so sweet. The kind of breast that a baby would learn to walk instantly to get a good sucking on! Man, the other side fell down and we now have two fucking breasts. Oh fucking a man I'm feeling good her folks this shit is WARMING UP!! Hell fucking yes. Now it was that stomach that just was a boner sight in its own!!! Then the belly button that you could put your tongue into and it wouldn't matter if it was full of lint.

Now was the real moment the boys had been waiting and watching for. The small lace thong hit the floor. As it did, the boys froze. Their dicks are harder than the hardest piece of oak. They could only witness this as a person watching a murder take place. Something so pure, but at the same time so unbelievably impure. The red lace girder was the last piece separating them from the most inexplicable joy a man has been given.

Fucking….yea the art of fucking I mean, come on, fucking brings a joy. An unbelievable pleasure, and I mean this sincerely. Some never experience it, even after 80 years of life or more. Yes, it is the purest feeling that requires the most intense act to receive. The melting of souls to the point of climax is what drives the fucking machine for the rest of that soul's existence. Only to chase the high that was experiencing an orgasm. Constantly chasing that rabbit again and again.

The only item remaining on her slowly slid, with the help of her seductive nails, down slowly from her hip, to the knee, and now to the ankles. As she bent over, the boys saw that finely manicured paradise. Yes, you know. Now it was all there. OMG, should they move in? Should they start fucking her???? Only to be that plank of oak, unmoved frozen-like pussy.

She crawled the length of that boy as a tigress would, almost like a prowl. As she reached his lips, she kissed and then nibbled. He couldn't move. This first boy was gifted in the piston department as she took his shirt and ripped it off, kissing his nipples. His piston began to rev up. She moved her well-manicured machine on his cock. His RPMs began to redline. She grabbed the buckle and positioned it between her skinny fingers, making sure her nails would rub his skin, and her cold fingers against his stomach to contrast the touch.

Miss Lacy was now as good as any skilled craftsman. She knew her craft very well. Something Suzy from English class could never bring. The craft of seduction. The belt popped open, and she pulled each leg of his pants one at a time, only to bring this group closer into her web. Only to have his Calvin Kleins stand as high as any respectable TeePee would.

She crawled back to that waistband, grabbing it with her teeth. All the other boys could do was pre-cumm their pants. She tugged, making sure her soft, seductive chin was rubbing the base pole of that teepee. She pulled those boxers off. Now we had two clean bodies, as designed in God's first original models, just skin; all items of clothing are gone. She maneuvered over that cock, slowly sliding the tip into her pussy. Gliding down its length, there was nothing left to absorb but his body. Uh oh….

Miss Lacy began to move her body at a rhythm that these boys had never seen. It was on. The boys got into action, and as they began to take everything off, she only turned and invited them. They all joined in. Oh fuck, yea party started! Man, this was soul train at its best chooo-choooo. As this symphony ensued, they echoed each other's actions, only for the conductor to orchestrate each one's turn over and over and over until each young man had emptied his load into her over and over, getting there monies worth? I mean nobody likes a sample platter for dinner?

As they lay there, she said she was going to the restroom to clean up. The boys started to giggle and to high-five each other. A while went by, then, as that imperfect square opened, the light let itself into the room. Blinding almost all of them. Fred entered, he wielded a machete. As she entered, it was a beautiful angel but she wielded a butcher's knife. The boys knew at that very second they would not be leaving the room 13; at least not the way they came in.

Androgynous in Color

As Miss Lacy walked in from the bathroom, the light beaming past her naked body, the boys froze. Fred grabbed the chairs at the table. Put them back-to-back in a T fashion. As Jonathan attempted to rise and make it to the door, he realized there were many deadbolts keyed from the inside. Shit. As he turned, he saw his friends all standing now, with Miss Lacy doing her rhythmic twirl humm, pointing for the boys to sit. Jonathan turned into Fred. Fred, being the piece of shit he was…now he was a terrifying machete-wielding piece of shit, so he walked slowly to his last and only chair. It was as if he were walking on Green Mile. Now, Miss Lacy, remember the hobbies section? Cutlery? She sat in a leather folder; it was bound.

Exotic Torture

As Jonathan awoke, there was a weird numbness in his right shoulder.

"Where the fuck am I?" He thought aloud.

As he slowly looked around, the room was a blur. He started to slowly gain focus. As he looked forward, he saw the lurch of Fred sitting on the bed. Knelt over him was Miss Lacy, fully sucking his cock.

It was erotic but terrifying at the same time. He turned to the left. He began to notice the pain in his right arm... What the fuck? His arm was gone. He started to move in a panic! As he did, his buddy awoke.

"Thomas, what the fuck, man?" Thomas was gurgling.

This wasn't fucking happening! Bbbbbbobby! Bbbooobbbyyyy!!!

As he tried to move, the restraints wouldn't allow it.

"Thomas…. Thomas!!!! ".

Nothing but gurgling and the slobber of Miss Lacy. She turned her gaze at him, smiling. if that's possible to do mid-blowjob! Ok, this is insane. Fred let a growl out as Miss Lacy released her Hoover-like motion as cumm filled her mouth.

Now her attention was on Jonathan. She stood, humming and twirling. As she arrived in front of Jonathan, she stopped and turned. Even at this moment, his cock began to fill. As he tried to stop it in disgust, all he could think was fucking her. She put herself on his cock. As she slid down on top of it, he could only feel her slippery pussy sliding down his cock. There is this feeling when pussy is wet that feels so good like a well lubricated hand. Just perfect.

She began to ride him as he sat in pain, unable to stop it. She raised a finger toward Fred. He came as the good boy he was. He came to Miss Lacy as a puppy would to a stick of jerky. He handed her a syringe. At this moment, he felt as if he was about to explode. He really did!!! All inside Miss Lacy. She arched and moaned. Fred took the needle and injected him full of meth.

Crazy Stripper

As his head filled with the drug, he felt as if his body were a rocket ship and Miss Lacy was the astronaut inside the capsule. She went to the table where the leather-bound torture kit sat.

She was shaking her hips back and forth. In such a motion that made it seem she was on a boat in the ocean, there was no gravity—almost a weightlessness to her motion. The pain was so intense that Jonathan's eyes began to water and welt. As the pain grew, it was as if it was replaced with the adrenaline and meth now running through his veins!

She grabbed her teddy and stockings and returned to the light of the bathroom that started it all. As the door closed, the darkness overwhelmed the entire room. As the lights of the city escaped through the tiny spaces of the windows and glowed throughout the room, he heard Fred. It was only a shadow, but he was there! As Jonathan turned, he saw Fred clearly. Now he had a blowtorch lit.

"WHAT THE FUCK?" Jonathan screamed as Fred took and applied a nice, ripe, dirty sock to Jonathan's mouth.

Now he was gagging and gurgling. Haha, that's a say it ten times fast as fuck saying?? GAGGING AND GURGLING... GAGGING AND GURGLING??? As the torch rang out as the only noticeable sound... Swish, the blade pierced the air. crack as it contacted Thomas' leg! The sound of the bone being pierced by the blade!

"No, no, no," Jonathan said under the gagging.

The gurgling stopped. Crack…. Crack…. The leg fell forward. All Thomas could do was pass the fuck out. Not Jonathan, he was as high as shit on meth. Watching in horror as his best friend was being cut up. The torch then hit the skin and began to cook the wound. Fred was good at doing Miss Lacy's bidding. She had taught him her skills as her previously being in the medical field. She knew exactly how inflict pain, but at the same time still keep her victims alive to continue the torture. At this moment, Miss Lacy opened the door. All dressed to kill. As she approached dancing and happy with the visions of pain on the boy's faces, she held the scalpel reflecting its shine into Bobby's eyes, knowing she was responsible for the whimpers of fear. All she could do was let her simple snicker and say "Run rabbit run …. Run rabbit run…. RUN RABBIT FUCKING RUN" As she danced in his presence. She moved around to Phillip also still humming and torturing? Haha Miss Lacy loves her Fear Factor!

Miss Lacy, as hot as hell in her red lace thong and Miss Lacy teddy, moved around to Bobby. She just chuckled her frail but violent self. Bobby began to soil himself. Miss Lacy pointed to Fred. Even Miss Lacy has her boundaries. Live shit is one. So, Fred grabbed Bobby and dragged him by his remaining one arm to the restroom. Back to sexy herself. She was sporting her favorite color RED! She enjoyed red.

Lipstick heels, fake wig RED,RED… she fucking loves red. Fred had Bobby over his shoulder and threw him down on a chair and tied him back up. Miss Lacy got in front of Bobby and took the scalpel slowly to cut his ankle wide fucking open!!! He screamed so loud. Mystery, no cops. Bobby totally passed out. When Bobby would wake up, his head was already drenched from the sweat. He started screaming aloud. Fred took another dirty, filthy sock to gag. As she arose, she began to dance, swaying like a ballerina on a Jenna Jameson set. She took Bobby's cock into her hand. As she did, it began to stiffen. She stood, took one of the Miss lacy arm sleeves, and slowly pulled it down in a twirl above her head, humming, and then the other. As she lowered, touching her ankles, her ass up, Bobby's cock was fully erect. She grabbed one stocking, then the other. As she turned...

Absolute Love of Misery

As Miss Lacy bent over, pulling the stockings down, Bobby's howl of pain excited her even more. She peeled each leg slowly, dancing to the tune inside her head! Fred stood to the attention of her command as the fucking lurch puppy he is. Blow torch in hand. Looking as creepy and lovely as his normal 6'7" ass could be. All the CheeseDick, a person would like to asszorb?!

Well, as Miss Lacy reached the end of her stocking show, she began to turn attention to Phillip. So far, Phillip has escaped her attention. She turned and slowly twisting and dancing. As she twirled, she slowly began to sing.

Twinkle Twinkle Little Fucking Star

How I wonder how fucked up you are

Up above the world so FUCKING HIGH

Twinkle Twinkle little star

HOW DEAD YOU FUCKING ARE!

As she grinned my Miss Lacy grin, laughing her her blood curdling laugh! She then gazed at Phillip, scalpel in hand.

Phillip was terrified. He began to cry, only fueling her glee! She took the scalpel down his thigh, being careful not to hit a vein. Now you must wonder how Miss Lacy knows where exactly to cut... I'm going to zap into her past. You see, Miss Lacy was once a normal human being.

Disastrous Roads

Ok, the beginning? So who was this evil b*tch? Well, let's rewind this fucked up weird ass clock. We are watching and following back to the disastrous road we are walking down. See, Miss Lacy is a product of our society. Pain and suffering are her companions for most. It was almost a rush. Same as the purest drug. It's only when all innocence is taken that you experience it. The problem is that now you have become a beast, and a beast devours. Once you become the beast, your devouring will eat all love, compassion, trust, and anything of the light. Your spectrum will become full of pain and suffering.

So here we go. Miss Lacy. She is a beast, a real tigress. At the age of five, her father, whom she trusted, decided to take advantage of that trust. As he went to her bedroom with evil intentions, he broke this trust to forever change Miss Lacy; to rape her innocence. As a father, he should burn at the stake? What he did to her for years would forever change her. To mold her into a beast of the society. As time passed, it darkened her soul.

One day at a time, pain and misery became normal. When something becomes normal, it no longer requires consequences. It becomes a routine. As she grew, she wanted to be a light in the darkness she was living in. She became a nurse to try and help people suffering. She went through medical school and aced it! A real genius. She could have easily become a doctor, but she chose nursing. Doctors heal bodies, nurses heal minds, and they show people compassion. That's what she wanted. Well, her first job was "Dunning Asylum," which was a psychiatric hospital. Well, what could go wrong here?

After the torture, evil begins.

So, Dunning is a really nice establishment. The kind you want to visit when you get a cold or sniffle...

This place has all the perks that a person loves in a rehabilitation clinic. Lobotomies, brain surgeries, electro-shock therapy, and my favorite chemical lab, human testing. As if a third eye or thumb isn't the coolest thing. Right?

Ok, back on topic. This place would make Frankenstein get chills. ……. Is that possible? Well, they liked to make Frankenstein copies here. This was your typical 24-hour torture clinic. Oh, they had the VIP section, "the Barn." Oh yeah, when you go there, you usually come out in multiple baggies! Kinda like a paper bag lunch like the Fred Flinstone one. Only this isn't Bedrock. Yaba Daba oh fuck you?

Well, our star, Miss Lacy, loved it. Not so much at first. She had to be broken in, like a pair of work boots. Uncomfortable at first, but then becomes second nature to your foot. They started for her in the tuberculosis unit. Oh yeah, nothing like watching an infant choke itself to death. Or a toddler suffocating.

Then she gradually worked up to the electroshock therapy unit. Well, this unit was quite shocking!. You know there are lots of transformers going on here! Man comes in…. a couple thousand volts to the brain. Bingo…. New man. Like most women wish they could do to their significant others secretly. Quite shocking?

Well, then she moved onto the lobotomies. Oh, yeah, the lobotomies. She was now getting really educated on the lifestyle. The heart went from light to dark in this joint. Oh yea. She was now transforming. Wait, that was the last unit? Oh, never mind. She was taking all that hatred and pain, and it was really spilling over here, kinda like tomato soup when it hits that crazy foaming stage. She was right where she needed to be.

This was her calling. She was now comfortable for the first time in her life. It was like that moment in college when you discovered 'this is what I want to be!' Well, she was in her own heaven. This school was the best for all of her soon-to-be perfect skill sets. So, onto biological and chemical testing. Let's not waste a lot of time here. That needs to be its own book. Well, now that we know where Miss Lacy got her training, we can better understand her, right? Moving on….

Four becomes three...

Ok, back to Phillip. She approaches him, wielding a scalpel. She motions for Fred, who walks over and holds Phillip's head. She began to do her humming and singing, but this time it was different.

London Bridge is falling down

Falling down, falling fucking down!

You hear me Phillip!

As she twirled the scalpel in the air as a conductor would leading his symphony into the dark of the night.

London Bridge is falling down

Falling fucking down

I am not your fair fucking lady tonight, Phillip!

She took the blade pointed it at Phillip. Fred held his head to make sure she held every second of his fear. As he was trembling, she began to stroke his cock. As she did, it began to rise. She whispered something into his ear that only the universe and Angel of Death understood. As Phillip looked forward, he quitted moving……She decided, for some weird reason, to end him quickly. She sat down on his cock slowly as Fred held his head forward. She did not ride his cock just slowly, moving rhythmically on it with the music in the background. She took the scalpel to his carotid artery, holding the knife not yet ready to end him. Phillip knew it was over as Miss Lacy slowly fucked him, he had accepted it. Miss Lacy became furious slicing his neck furiously and riding his cock now. As she cut violently, blood spilled everywhere, squirting up out all over covering Jonathan, Bobby, and Thomas. Miss Lacy arched as she finished her climax looking into Phillips now lifeless eyes. She stood up with blood dripping off her grin as she walked around her remaining victims, smiling like a Cheshire Cat. She went to the lit bathroom. As she was shutting the door, she looked back, pointing at Jonathan. She snapped her fingers. Fred, then... ok, let's talk about where "the lurch" came from.

Mommy is the best.

So let's dive into the dark past of Fred. He was always a big lurch of a kid. He was 6 when his father died. His mother was a real peach. His father was a decent guy and he worked at the local sawmill. His mother, on the other hand, was a real piece of shit. By the time Daddy's lunch bell had rung, she had probably gobbled down a full bottle of pills, sucked four cocks and probably free based enough shit to drop an elephant. By dinner bell, she had probably fucked her pusher, her neighbor, and probably fucked the paper boy as well. Well, she dabbled in the fine arts of crack, glass, and a large portion of whatever's available. Well, Daddy knew what was going on, so one day he slipped in the back door. He was going to put his foot down. Ok, let's see drugs and drug dealers. This was Betty Crocker's recipe for a "pushing up daisy" dish.

Only today's fate had an extra pinch of fuck up, Daddy. He walked into mommy dearest, taking the L train. As he stood there, Mack Daddy Curtis grabbed his pistol and laid out the final part of this recipe. The final act of Fred's senior. memoir. So that's that. Now mommy was unleashed, and she was a pit bull.

So, poor innocent Fred JR was about to be the object of mommy's satanic cult of personality. Well, when he reached 15 and was already pushing six feet six, well, mommy loved her some fresh cock, so she took advantage of her son's girth. Whoever saw this coming? Raise those hands. Yes, you saw this coming?

So she put a nightly dose of her love on this monster. As he learned the craft of fucking, he took after Mommy and found his prey. She was a local girl. Well, Fred JR did everything a full cheesedick would. Well, word got out after what happened, and the local law enforcement agency showed up, took his ass into custody, and sent him off to Dunning. There, he was a patient of these dark arts and learned the blackness he was destined to become…..

I wish I had a leg up.

Well, now we can see the levels of evil we are talking about here. Fred and Miss Lacy were well-manicured torture and murder experts. They were definitely seasoned terror experts. As Fred approached, he stood above Jonathan, machete in hand. As all 325 pounds hovered above him. It was a moment that would have made a grizzly bear stop and take notice. For some unknown reason, Fred was almost scared of Jonathan. Was it because of Miss Lacy, or was it that Fred was just fucking stupid? Only inside the fat cock suckers head was the answer to that question.

As he stood there motionless, Jonathan took his foot as hard as he could and kicked him in his balls. There was a grunt. That's it? He turned toward Thomas. As he did, it was so quiet, except for the singing of Miss Lacy and Fred's labored breathing. The flickering of the city's lights through the window, the window that represented freedom that none would have! Not even the lovebirds. Oh shit, did I just give a piece of this journey's end?! Maybe, maybe not.

So as Fred towered over Thomas, Thomas began to piss on himself. It might as well have been Niagara Falls at this point; it was so silent. Then, out of nowhere, Fred went into a rage, cracking Thomas skull wide open. As the blade hit his skull, Jonathan watched in a frozen awe. The blade got stuck, and the blood slowly streamed down his face.

As Jonathan watched in horror, his friend's eyes, still able to move, looked into Jonathan. His eyes began to go dark. His pupils were so solid black that they no longer had life. As Fred put his size 14 boot on Thomas' chest to release the blade, it made a swoosh sound, but no blood was squirting more of a dibble, the same as Thomas' lifeless body slumped forward. Now there were only two victims left. Jonathan and Bobby. Now Bobby. He was not mentioned here in this story. Well, let's see...

Robert Monsanto

Ok, Bobby. He was your typical kid. Growing up, he had a very suburban, sheltered life. He was 12 when he saw his first naked woman. Whoever you ask, it was his 17-year-old cousin. She was staying with the Monsantos because she was a troubled child. Her father raped and abused her. Her Xanax mother held little control over or even cared for anything hardly anyone. She was a perfect storm for Bobby. She had bad baggage. She had been expelled from every school in LA, so her Xanax mother and sticky fingers father devised a plan to ship her to Chicago. As she arrived, it was Bobby's first time to see mini skirts or halter tops. Oh, she had it all. Tits an ass that slipped under her mini skirt's edge. This started Bobby's destiny—to bring him here to Miss Lacy. The Devil in Red Lipstick.

So, Bobby decided to be a creepy pervert one Saturday evening while his cousin was showering and snuck in. Under the cover of the mist of steam, he pulled down his pants and began to stroke his cock. Ok, mind you, he has not even dropped balls yet. So this was like watching a fentanyl addict wake up from his stupor. Ok, we won't spend too much energy here because we have all been here. Whether you are 12 or 50, you had playfully enjoyed such thing. So, his elbow hit a bottle on the sink. "Clunk," it hit the rug, and he froze. Ok, he's in a tiny bathroom. It's like the elephant who thought the tree would hide him. Really. Yes, he froze with Dick in hand. "Oh, Shit!" was his only thought! So as the "clunk" happened, it turned to "clink chhhhhhhhhhhhhaaadund" as it rolled to the porcelain tub. "Fuck, fuck, fuck, maybe she didn't hear it?" Nope, no such luck? Swooosh, the curtain opened. Ok, this is a moment in life to live in infamy.

the moment of standing in front of your cousin with your hard dick in your hand.

As they both stood there, she began to smile. What the fuck was happening? She motioned for him. Well, of course, this was a no-brainer. He hoped in the shower. She grabbed his cock and began to stroke it. He felt paralyzed. She just giggled. Then he went from being a kid…. to being a man in a millisecond! He grabbed her hair, spun her around, and took his exploding cock, shoving it in her like he knew exactly what he was doing. She arched right into him. She was moaning now at his fucking. Bobby began to thrust harder, and she fucking let a whale of a scream out. Fuck me, Bobby! Fuck me. He was about to blow his shit, then she turned around, went to her knees, and took him into her mouth until he filled her with everything he had!! She moaned while his body stiffened. As she rose, she turned the water off, grabbed her towel, and walked out, wagging her ass like a proud older cousin!

To the bathroom again!?

Thomas was just executed; just Bobby and Jonathan left now! Miss Lacy walked out, and Fred froze!!

Well, Miss Lacy was in there awhile. What the fuck was so incredibly interesting in there? Was there a fourth-dimensional room there? Like Doctor Who's phone booth? I mean, what were they doing with their bodies already? So, Fred's frozen Bobby has soiled himself. Jonathan is pissed off. Here comes Miss Lacy, only that now she's very bloody and very naked. What's going to happen here? Only she can tell. Was she going to kill someone? Was she going to fuck someone? Let's find out, shall we?

As Miss Lacy approached, you could hear a cricket fart. For such a terrifying killer, she had the softest walk a person could possibly have. I mean, perfect heel-to-toe movement. Can you hear that? No, you cannot. She was as silent as a cat. Methodically moving without a sound and as graceful as a gentle breeze. She walked toward the window and stopped. As she gazed outside, holy sh*t, she spoke. For the first time in, like, forever, she spoke. She said in a very motherly voice, "Jonathan?". She paused, gazing out the window. "Do you know it's no mistake you're here?" She asked. As Jonathan heard this, his mind began to race. What the fuck was this b*tch talking about? "Jonathan, listen to me as I tell you a story," she said. Ok, this shit's getting wild. Are we about to hear about Miss Lacy's motives for all this madness?

A Child Born of Wedlock

Ok, let's see if Miss Lacy is becoming a calm Socrates for us. I'm confused, but intellectually intrigued. What was going on? Well, let's find out, shall we? As she spoke, it was so tense that a priest would cringe.

So she said, "There was a young girl I once knew. She was born of wedlock, then carried, then brought into this world. As this child was delivered, she was cruel and insane. She grew to have a child too. It was a son, a special son." As she continued, Jonathan knew exactly what was going on. Miss Lacy was his grandmother! What the fuck? Oh shit, no wonder Fred would not touch him. He heard Miss Lacy continue. "Your mother was my child, Jonathan." She kept her gaze outside. She continued, "Jonathan, you see, this night was to test and see." She turned and motioned to Fred. They went toward Bobby.

The Last of the torture

Bobby gazed, sitting in his own shit and pissing his tear ducts empty. Fred was standing with his machette in hand, and Miss Lacy was all pretty and ready to fuck. She motioned to Fred. Fred threw Bobby over his shoulder and took him to the restroom. Bobby was there for an eternity. All you could hear was Bobby's screams. The door opened, Fred took Bobby to Thomas' chair and sat him down. His mouth had been sewn shut. Miss Lacy moved in. She grabbed Bobby's manhood, and began to stroke it as he whimpered quietly, trying not to enjoy it. It began to rise as Fred took a clear bag out. Miss Lacy looked at Fred. He took Jonathan's chair and turned it around to put Bobby and Jonathan face-to-face. Then, Fred walked behind Bobby. As Miss Lacy took Bobby's cock into her mouth, Fred slipped the bag over his head. His breaths began to increase. As she sucked his cock, Bobby couldn't help but breathe heavily.

As Jonathan watched, there was nothing he could do. Bobby has now started to wiggle back and forth, and as his cock exploded, it was his last breath. Fred took the bag off. His head fell forward. Miss Lacy snapped her fingers. Fred untied Bobby's limp body. He threw him over his back and took him to the fourth dimension. Then Miss Lacy stood, grabbed the chair and slid it forward. As she sat, Jonathan became terrified.

Moments of Remorse

She sat there, staring at Jonathan. She started to say, "Let's talk, kiddo." She walked over to the table and grabbed the scalpel and red lipstick. As she returned, she was humming the tune "Little Miss Muffet Song.".

"Little miss Muffet she sat on her tuffet, eating her curds and whey" she sang very calmly. "Along came a spider who sat down beside her" as she began to sit down. She sat and stared into Jonathan's eyes. Jonathan could feel the evil radiating from her. It was so strong he was actually getting angry!! He had enough of this shit! As he started to tell her to fuck off, she took the red lipstick and started to apply it. There was this magnetic attraction she radiated also through her terror. She smiled, crossed her legs provocatively and applying that red lipstick. One armed Jonathan had no choice but to be turned on?

What the fuck was going on? His head was spinning, all emotions running wild! She then took her leg off the other so that her pussy was visible from the red laced panties. She continued the lipstick….moving her knees back and forth as if to draw attention to her pussy. She capped the lipstick. Jonathan was as hard as a rock now. She motioned to Fred. He walked to the table where a Radio was on. He pushed play. A song began to play. Revolting Cocks "da ya think I'm sexy". As provocative as this was, this song was pushing it over the top. She stood up and came to Jonathan now.

As Jonathan sat there thinking about his life, his friends, and now this extremely exotic woman dancing in front of him. She was really stunning in her ability to make a jman forget his ambitions, his morality and open to his primal instincts. As he sat there tied up, she continued to dance for him. All his regrets and ambitions in life slipping away as the sand in an hourglass. Miss Lacy came over to him and sat on his thighs, facing him. She took the gag from his mouth and began to kiss him seductively. All his moments of remorse were slowly being drained. She continued kissing him slowly, seductively and passionately. The red lipstick transferred to him. She took her hand down his chest, down his cock. Cold and almost soft was her hands on his hard hot intense cock. She took it in her hand. Jonathan was now motionless, like a piece of putty to Miss Lacy's gaze. Only to fall once again as every man before him, as she knew he was unable to fight any longer. She started to remove his restraints. She took his single hand leading him to the bed. As he stood before this magnificent specimen of a woman, she gently pushed his chest. He fell backwards, never losing eye contact, as if she was pushing him into a cloud high in the sky. She knelt on one knee, then the other over his own knees. Then putting one hand, then the other on his waist as she moved slowly to her knees fully on the bed. She was moving as playfully as a cat. Jonathan could only feel lust and desire. She moved forward onto him. As she made her way over him, his breathing was now labored. She knew she had him exactly where she wanted. She removed her lace. She climbed onto him and started moving rhythmically with the music, and all he could do was enjoy her. This was almost insane in his mind but part of him felt it was as natural as riding a bike; she stayed on him after finishing her pleasures with him. She played with his hair as a mother would. So peaceful. She started to tell him a story….

The World's Demise

"So Jonathan that was fun right?" All he could do was say "yes".

"Ok Jonathan I want to tell you why your feelings are so very strong for me and our melting as one." She said.

This story is one that is about to leave you fucking speechless! Ok, as she spoke, Jonathan felt as if he knew this all along. He knew it to be true. So she began to tell him.

You see, Miss Lacy is millions of years old. Her true being is mixed in with the human soul. What is a soul? Is it some bright light? Is it like Casper the friendly ghost? Is it a Jeannie in a bottle? Is it simply electrons flowing in an organic nervous system firing as a reaction just as a nucleus does in an atomic bomb? Well I don't know. But folks, I know what Miss Lacy is. As she said, millions of years old. Let's listen to her explain it way more fun!

So Miss Lacy laid there with Jonathan and began this part of this insane story's ultimate twist. You ask yourself millions of years old. Oh, the bathroom? The entire night? Why? Here she goes in her theatrical manner!

"Jonathan you see your blood is partly mine" "you see your mother is my child" she told him. " I am a traveler from another world, we feed on another's world's energy." As she was explaining, let me jump back real quick.

The Queen's Beginning

So let's rewind back to Dunning. You remember that lovely place. The hospital that sends out body parts like sack lunches yabba dabba dooo. Well let's talk a bit more here. So, Miss Lacy completed her medical school ... .mind you she was acing it…. She had no desire to be a doctor though. She wanted to be a nurse. To change the world. What she didn't know was she was on a path to do just that! As she was walking down the street, she stumbled upon a gentleman. OMG, it was him! The one she felt so attracted to! As she walked, she felt it! She was over five hundred steps away but she could feel his hands on her hips and his lips upon hers. He was so magical. As those steps turned to 400 now as he stood at the bus stop, she could only feel his magnetism just pulling her like a tractor beam from Star Wars. Now 350, her heart beat began to increase. 300 hundred: her chest was beating faster and faster. Now 250! His beauty was becoming clearer. His chin was perfect. His physique was that of a god. Ok, now the steps were getting shorter and shorter until they were less than 100. What was she to do? He had not even noticed her. Oh my! Her hands were sweating and her body was shaking. She felt as if she was going to just collapse. Now, she was so close she had to choose: was she going to keep walking or was she going to get onto a bus she had no idea where it was going to? Just to buy more time to have him notice her? 10,9,8,7,6, nothing. The bus pulled up and he stepped aboard. 5,4 her mind was racing. She could not let him go as if he was a drug. She had to be high. 3,2, she was going to fucking explode! 1 on the bus she went. As she looked, he was the only one on the bus.

She realized she was now being drawn forward by an unexplained force. Each step and she felt lightning bolts were striking her and pushing her. As she now stood so close to him, she could feel his breath on her forehead as he grabbed her on each cheek, gliding her mouth to his. It was a stick of TNT in his pants. She could feel it was so close. She began to rub it as he smiled and said, "patience my love". She was almost about to explode! She held him so tight that her nails were digging into his back. He told her his apartment was around the corner and she agreed. As they stepped off the bus, she literally had no idea her fate was literally changing forever. As they walked, her anticipation was peaking. Who was he? Why was he so intoxicating? She walked the steps to his apartment not knowing that she had to die to be reborn as the king's queen.

He took her inside and had her sit. He went to the cabinet to grab the glasses and an ancient stern of wine. He poured the wine. As he did, he asked her: "Would you die for me?" All she could do was to nod "yes". He then said, "then drink". As she drank the most bitter wine she had ever drunk, she almost instantly felt it coarse her veins. As it did, she felt her throat slowly closing. She couldn't breathe. She felt her soul slipping into darkness. As she reached for him, she fell forward into him. As she was falling, the room's lights were fading…..

Queen Has Risen

She felt her eyes opening. She couldn't focus as she looked over. There was no one there? She was in her own apartment. Was it all a dream? She felt different, almost like she was full of energy. She looked at her clock, oh shit, it was 10am and she had a test in 30 minutes. She hurried to the closet and grabbed her clothes. As she put her new panties on, she saw blood on the old ones. She wasn't due for a period in days. Was she spotting? Well she threw on her school dress and powder. Oh yea, today was a hat day! As she was rushing, she ran into the homeless man we discussed earlier. He informed her of Dunning. So, she went to her test.

She felt as if she was being driven into a situation. You know the gut feelings you get when you are about to leave the platform on a roller coaster? Well, she was feeling that. She finished her test and got on the train but it took her to another station instead of going to the desired stop. She fell asleep and woke at the Dunning stop. What the fuck was going on? As she walked out of the train, it was dark. The only light was radiating from the hospital. So, she decided to call her friend to inform her of her mistake. As she entered, it was empty. No staff to be seen. She walked the hallway and the beds were empty? What was going on here? Did something happen that she did not know about?

She traveled the hallway forward to the bright light as if she was being driven. She walked through the door into a operating room. As she went through the double doors, she saw a corpse on a gurney? There were the staff, all kneeling and Mr right standing in a doctor's uniform. As she walked forward, the staff began to humm a really familiar song. One she felt she had heard before. Mr Right, John, said "come Miss Lacy and receive your gift". As she walked forward, a tall obscene looking man walked in behind her. She started to run but she realized this was futile. She kept walking. John said "lie down" pointing to the empty gurney.

"Oh, no!" She had no choice but to do as told? She lay down. He took a saw out as the beast of a man held her as Mr wonderful cut her arm off! She took it as if it was like getting a tooth pulled. The beast took a torch and sealed the wound as the chemical was administered. It felt like speed racing through her veins. Then, at that moment she knew. She had died the night before. That was why the blood was in her underwear. They had taken her eggs to produce the child. The child - Lucinda - Jonathan's mother? The king had to be born but molded again. It was the way.

They took the arm from the corpse and sewn it onto her? The queen was born! …..

The Kings Final Transformations

As we return to this fucked up situation at room 13 in Akbars Grand Motel on that lonely street corner in a dark Chicago night! As we wind this one down or up is up to you. As the reader, I ask you one question: what do you want? That being said, you take this ending and take our Miss Lacy wherever you want to take her. Now, she will have her king so there is nothing she cannot become or do. So, as Jonathan heard her story now, he knew what was happening. He remembered everything. Last week when he visited this place and drank from the stern, life and death were the same. It was time. As Fred and his friends came out of the bathroom, Fred was carrying the corpse and laid it on the floor and knelt as did what once was Thomas, Bobby and Phillip. All kneeling before their king and queen. Lucinda was also here now. The whole fucking family!! Fred grabbed the corpse's arm and ripped it off to sew it onto Jonathan.

Once empty now place on his shoulder. Jonathan could feel the power racing in his veins. As he did before. Now the darkness was flowing through his soul, it was consuming his soul. As a person with bowl of ice cream. The arm was molding vein were growing. He began to rise the dark knight was finally risen as he rose energy was emitting two horns grew and wings began to flip. The beast was one with Jonathan. The light was so bright. Fred, the rest could only look down, the energy would consume them. As he did it began to mold to his body. As he began to stand, the transformation was completed. He was now the king they waited all these years, millions of them to finally have before them. As he stood, his wings spread and the light radiated as bright as the brightest star.

The End

Or the beginning you Decide?

BIOGRAPHY

Jimmy Swagger

Born on September 28, 1975, in Alaska, Jimmy entered this world. At the age of 5, his family relocated to Arkansas due to his father's military service, resulting in a strict upbringing. Unfortunately, at the tender age of 7, he experienced the loss of his beloved grandfather, which plunged his family into turmoil. At the age of 13, Jimmy resorted to car theft. He was passionate about skateboarding and other activities. When he turned fifteen, his abusive father abandoned him, sending him to live with his father's brother in Michigan. During his time there, with no access to television, Jimmy found solace in reading, which became a significant part of his isolated life. Upon his return, he discovered that his younger brother had fallen into drug addiction and had been arrested. Witnessing his brother's struggle served as a turning point for Jimmy, deterring him from substance abuse. However, he sought refuge in alcohol, enduring immense pain and torment throughout his life.

Despite his troubled past, Jimmy managed to establish a career as an electrician and later as an electrical engineer. His profession allowed him to travel extensively, but his alcoholic lifestyle caused him to burn bridges along the way, ultimately leading to the end of his first marriage. Despite this setback, Jimmy became a father to two children before divorcing and continuing to battle the demons within him. During this tumultuous period, he encountered a woman who later fell ill, and together they had another child. They faced numerous challenges and eventually Jimmy found himself imprisoned for defrauding the government. It was during his time in prison that he discovered the power of writing. The darkness of his environment seeped into his words, shaping his writing style.

And now, we find ourselves here, with Jimmy as the author of his own story. He has been on a journey of sobriety for nearly two years, overcoming his struggles and embracing a new chapter in his life.

www.ingramcontent.com/pod-product-compliance
Lightning Source LLC
Chambersburg PA
CBHW040843010826
48978CB00012BB/873